LIKE PICKLE JUICE ON A COOKIE

LIKE PICKLE JUICE ON A COOKIE

BY JULIE STERNBERG

ILLUSTRATIONS BY MATTHEW CORDELL

Amulet Books, New York

The Library of Congress has catalogued the hardcover edition of this book as follows:

Sternberg, Julie
Like pickle juice on a cookie / by Julie Sternberg ; illustrated by Matthew Cordell.
p. cm.
Summary: When nine-year-old Eleanor's beloved babysitter Bibi moves away to care for her ailing father, Eleanor must spend the summer adjusting to a new babysitter while mourning the loss of her old one.
ISBN 978-0-8109-8424-0
[1. Novels in verse. 2. Babysitters—Fiction. 3. Loss (Psychology)—Fiction. 4. Self-reliance—Fiction.] I. Cordell, Matthew, 1975– ill. II. Title.
PZ7.5.S74 Li 2011
[Fic]—dc22
2009015975

ISBN for this edition: 978-1-4197-2050-5

Text copyright © 2011 Julie Sternberg
Illustrations copyright © 2011 Matthew Cordell
Book design by Melissa Arnst

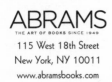

THE ART OF BOOKS SINCE 1949
115 West 18th Street
New York, NY 10011
www.abramsbooks.com

TO MY GRANDMOTHER, BABE, WITH LOVE

—J. S.

CHAPTER ONE

I had a bad August.

A very bad August.

As bad as pickle juice on a cookie.

As bad as a spiderweb on your leg.

As bad as the black parts of a banana.

I hope your August was better.

I really do.

CHAPTER TWO

My bad time started one morning
when my parents sat down in my room.
"We have some difficult news," they said.
I hate it when they say that.
It means they have terrible news.
Just rotten.
The last time they had difficult news,
they had lost my hamster.
Her name was Dr. Biggles.
My dad had left her cage open.
We went from door to door
in our Brooklyn apartment building.
We asked all the neighbors,
"Have you seen Dr. Biggles?"

But we never found her.

I tried to think what news could be as difficult as that.

"Did Grandma Sadie die?" I asked.

"Of course not!"

said my mother.

"Grandma Sadie is in excellent health,"

said my father.

"Why would you ask such a question?"

said my mother.

"She is the oldest person I know," I said.

"I thought she might have died.

That would be difficult news."

My mother shivered.

"Yes," she said.

"That would be very difficult news."

"Nobody died,"

my father said.

CHAPTER THREE

"So what is the news?" I asked.

My father looked at my mother.

My mother took a deep breath.

"Bibi is moving away," she said.

I blinked at them.

I could not speak.

Bibi is my babysitter.

She has been my babysitter my whole life.

She is the best babysitter in the world.

She makes me soup when I am sick.

She holds my feet when I do handstands.

She knows which of my teeth are loose

and which ones I've lost
and where I was when I lost them.
She rubs my back when I am tired.
She takes a needle and thread
and sews up my pants
to make them fit right.
And she knows not to tickle me.
Because I hate to be tickled.

"Bibi cannot move away," I said.
"She is moving to Florida," my father said.
"To be with her father.
He is sick.
He needs her."
"*I* need her," I said.
"Bibi cannot move away," I said again.
"You are eight, Eleanor," my mom said.
"You are getting so big.
You don't need Bibi as much as you used to.

Everything will be okay."

I started to cry.

"I don't want to get so big," I said.

"Everything will *not* be okay," I said.

"This is as bad as somebody dying," I said.

And it was.

It was as bad as somebody dying.

CHAPTER FOUR

We had a going-away party for Bibi.

All of her friends came.

Angela and Connie and Blossom and Dee.

Everyone gave her presents.

Except for me.

I could not make Bibi a good-bye present.

Or pick one out.

My mom gave Bibi a picture of me in a pretty frame.

Bibi said she would keep it by her bed

so she could see me when she woke up

and when she went to sleep.

Everybody at that party cried.

My dad cried.

My mom cried.

Angela and Connie and Blossom and Dee cried.

Bibi cried.

And I cried.

I cried a lot.

It was not a fun party.

I hope you never go to a party like that.

I really do.

CHAPTER FIVE

At the end of the party,
Bibi put her presents in big shopping bags.
Then it was time for her to go.
"Maybe we shouldn't all go outside with Bibi,"
my dad said.
"It will be very sad outside."
"It's sad inside," I said.
"I want to go," I said.
So we all went.
My parents helped Bibi get a cab.
Then we hugged her
and she hugged us
and she climbed into the cab
and pulled the door shut

and turned toward us
and the cab drove off.
And now I know the worst thing in the world.
The worst thing in the world
is a cab
driving farther and farther away
with Bibi in the backseat
waving good-bye.

CHAPTER SIX

The next morning I woke up
and wrapped myself in my blanket
and went in the living room
and sat on the sofa
and waited
for the sound of Bibi's key in the door.
I knew I wouldn't hear Bibi's key in the door.
But still
I thought
maybe.
Maybe she forgot something.
Maybe she changed her mind.
Maybe her dad got well.

So I waited
and listened
and waited
and waited
until my mom came in
and sat beside me
and held me tight.
"This feels just awful," she said.
We sat there together
feeling awful.
Then she said,
"Should we have something special for breakfast?
Some chocolate-chip pancakes?"
"No," I said.
"With powdered sugar?"
"No," I said.
"Cinnamon toast with extra cinnamon?"
"No," I said.

"How about pickle juice on a cookie?" she said.

"Would you like pickle juice on a cookie?"

And then I had to smile.

Because that was just ridiculous.

CHAPTER SEVEN

After Bibi left, my mom took a little time off from work.

"We'll get through this together," she said.

But there were lots of things we could not do.

We could not call Bibi,

because she was away,

at the hospital,

taking care of her sick father.

We could not call Grandma Sadie, either.

Because Grandma Sadie

would ask me about Bibi.

We could not go to Roma Pizza.

Because Bibi loved Roma Pizza.

So Roma Pizza reminded me of Bibi.

We could not ride my bike.

Because Bibi helped pick out my bike.

So my bike reminded me of Bibi.

We could not go swimming at the gym.

Because Bibi was scared of swimming.

So swimming reminded me of Bibi.

Sometimes

after I told my mom what we could not do

she would ask,

"Is there anything that we *can* do?"

So I would let her read to me.

And bake cookies with me.

And take me to the Flatbush Avenue diner.

Because I didn't want her to get too cranky.

CHAPTER EIGHT

One day,
after breakfast,
my mom said,
"I have to make a work call now.
I'm very sorry.
I wish I didn't have to,
but it's an important call.
I'm afraid you'll have to be quiet.
And you can't interrupt."
Then she picked up the phone
and started dialing.

That call went on forever.

Finally I pulled on her sleeve.
"Will you ever be done?"
I whispered.

She frowned at me
and shook her head at me
and put her finger to her lips.

That meant no.
She would never be done.

I left her there
on her very important call
and decided to look through her clothes.

I like looking through her clothes.
I tried on her long black dress
with beads on the straps
and her highest-heeled shoes.
Then I opened a dresser drawer,
my favorite dresser drawer,
full of fancy scarves.
Grandma Sadie sends my mom those scarves.
I took them out one by one
and unfolded them
and set them down
until I got to the navy one
that's covered with cherries.

Bibi loves cherries.

Before she moved away,
we used to sit at the kitchen table
with a bowl for me
and a bowl for her
and a bowl in the middle for the pits.
We'd eat all those cherries
and spit out the pits.
Bibi would always remind me
not to swallow the pit.
And I never did.
I never swallowed a single pit.

I didn't ask my mom if I could have her navy scarf
that's covered with cherries.
I just took it
and hid it under my pillow
and decided to keep it there forever.

CHAPTER NINE

After her very important call
my mom sat on the couch with me
and read five whole chapters of a book to me.
She didn't even stop when the phone rang.
"We'll let the machine get it," she said.
And when we got to the happy ending,
my mom's eyes got red
and her cheeks got blotchy.
"Are you crying?" I asked.
She laughed and touched her eyes.
"I guess I am," she said.
"I always do."
It's true.
My mom always cries at happy endings.

All of a sudden,
as I was watching her cry,
I glanced at her neck,
where she sometimes wears a fancy scarf.
My own face got hot
and my heart felt funny.

I jumped up.

"Wait right here," I said.
"I'll be right back."

Then I ran to my room
and threw aside my pillow
and grabbed the cherry scarf,
which looked a little crumpled.
I smoothed it as best as I could
against the top of my leg
and ran to my mom's room

and pulled open the drawer
and folded the scarf
and slipped it in
near the middle of the stack
and closed the drawer fast
but tried not to slam it
and ran back to my mom.

I was breathing fast.

I tried to stop breathing fast.
I tried to look perfectly normal.

My mom raised her eyebrows at me.
"What's going on?" she asked.
"Nothing," I said.
"Are you sure?" she asked.
"I'm sure," I said.
Then,

hoping to distract her,

I said,

"Can we make some grilled cheese?"

It was the perfect distraction.

"I love grilled cheese," my mom said.

We went into the kitchen.

And as I watched her take the bread

and the cheese

and the butter

out of the refrigerator

I decided

that I never wanted to see

another fancy scarf

again.

CHAPTER TEN

The next Sunday,
as my mom was leaving to visit her aunt,
my dad came into my room.
"Guess who I just saw in the lobby?" he asked.
He looked very happy.
I couldn't think of a neighbor
who would make him so happy.
So I said,
"Jorge Posada?"

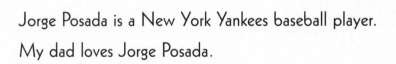

Jorge Posada is a New York Yankees baseball player.
My dad loves Jorge Posada.

My dad laughed.

"It wasn't Jorge," he said.

"Then who?" I asked.

"Agnes," he said.

"From the apartment upstairs.

She was there with her mom.

I invited her to come play with you.

And she's coming!"

My mouth dropped open

and I sat straight up

and I started shaking my hands at my dad.

"I don't like Agnes from upstairs!" I said.

"You don't?" he said.

He didn't look happy anymore.

"No!" I said.

"I don't!"

Agnes from upstairs is scary.

She never talks to me.

Or smiles.
And one time,
in the lobby,
near the doorman's desk,
she jumped on her brother
and they both fell on my feet
and I tripped over them
and landed hard on my arm.
Bibi was there.
She helped us up
and fussed at them.

"You see all these people," she said,

wagging her finger at them.

"You can't be so wild."

Then she brought Agnes and her brother to their dad

and took me upstairs

and put ice in a bag

and laid a towel on my arm

and held the ice

on the towel

on my arm

for a good long time.

I liked sitting there,

with Bibi holding ice on my arm.

So I never told her

that before she even started

my arm was feeling fine.

I said to my dad,

"I don't want to play with Agnes."

"But your friend Pearl is away,"
he said.
"So many of your friends are away.
And I want you to have fun.
Summer is supposed to be fun."
"Agnes is not fun," I said.
"Oh dear," my dad said. "I'm not sure what to do."
He looked worried.
"Call her mom," I said.
"Tell them not to come."
"But Agnes might feel very hurt," my dad said.
I glared at him.
He still looked worried.
Finally I said,
"If Agnes is coming over,
you have to stay with me.
The *whole* time."
"I will," he said. "I promise."

CHAPTER ELEVEN

A little while later the doorbell rang.

Agnes was there with her mom.

"We should do this all the time!"

her mom said.

Agnes didn't say anything.

I didn't say anything.

"Come in!"

my dad said.

"Come in!"

So Agnes came in.

"I'm right upstairs if you need me!"

her mom said.

Then she left.

"Have a seat, you two!"

my dad said.

"Have a seat!"

I pulled on his arm.

"Stop saying everything twice,"

I whispered.

"Oh!"

he whispered back.

"Sorry!"

We all sat down on the couch.

"Aren't you both eight?"

my dad asked.

"No!" I said.

Agnes still didn't say anything.

"She's nine," I said.

"So you've already been through third grade!"

my dad said.

"How perfect!

Eleanor is starting third grade soon.

You can tell us all about it."

He waited.

We both waited.

Finally Agnes said,

"It's okay."

"Do you write any stories in third grade?

I used to love to write stories," my dad said.

"Yes,"

Agnes said.

"We wrote stories.

And letters.

Other things, too, I guess.

I can't remember."

I can write stories and letters,

I thought.

We did that in second grade.

And then I thought,

Letters!

I can write letters!

And then I stood up.

"I'm going to write a letter," I said.
"Right now?"
my dad asked.
"Right now,"
I said.
"Would you like to write a letter, too?"
my dad asked Agnes.
"No thanks," she said.
Then she said,
"Could I listen to some music?"
My dad looked surprised.
"Sure," he said.

So my dad took Agnes to look through our music.

I got my best stationery
and I sharpened a pencil.
Then I sat down at the kitchen table.
And I wrote a letter to Bibi.

I wrote:

Dear Bibi,

Agnes from upstairs is here.

Dad invited her.

He didn't ask me first.

Don't worry.

She is being very calm.

Yesterday Mom bought me new pants.

So I will have them for school.

They're too big.

Nobody here can sew except for you.

And you left.

So I have to wear a belt.

Here is a picture of me in my too-big pants.

And here is a picture of calm Agnes on our sofa.

I miss you every single day. I really do.

And I love you a million trillion.

Love,

Eleanor

I didn't want Agnes to see my letter.

Because it was private.

And she might feel funny.

Since I wrote about her.

So I folded it up right away

and pushed it in an envelope

and wrote my return address in the corner.

Just like we did in second grade.

Then I went to find my dad,

to get Bibi's address.

He was standing with Agnes by the stereo.

They were singing a Beatles song.

My dad does not sing very well.

But Agnes from upstairs sounded beautiful.

My dad smiled at me.

"Want to sing with us?" he asked.

"No thanks," I said.

"I need Bibi's address."

So my dad got Bibi's address

while Agnes sang.

I liked listening to Agnes sing.

But I was ready for her to go home.

Finally,

as she went upstairs with her mom,

I went downstairs with my dad.

And I mailed my letter to Bibi.

CHAPTER TWELVE

As soon as my mom came home I told her,
"I wrote a letter to Bibi."
"That's nice," she said.
But I could tell she wasn't really listening.
She sat down on the couch
and patted the space next to her.
So I sat down beside her.
"I have to go back to work soon," she said.
"We need to find someone to help us.
Someone to be with you during the daytime
until the end of summer
and then pick you up from school
when third grade starts."

"I don't want a new babysitter," I said.

"I understand that," my mom said.

"I really do.

But we don't have a choice.

Your dad and I both work."

"I could stay by myself," I said.

"No," my mom said.

"You really couldn't."

I knew that.

But still.

"I won't like anyone else," I said.

"I understand," my mom said.

"No one in the world
is as good as Bibi," I said.

"I know," my mom said.

"But maybe we can find someone
who is not too terrible.

I heard about someone named Natalie.

Maybe we could try her out."

"Do we have to?" I asked.

"We have to," my mom said.

"Fine," I said.

But I didn't like it.

CHAPTER THIRTEEN

Natalie came over that very afternoon.
"You keep inviting people without asking me,"
I told my dad.
But he wasn't listening.
He was opening the door for Natalie.

Natalie didn't look anything like Bibi.
She looked much younger.
She had a ponytail.
Bibi did not have a ponytail.
Natalie wore jeans.
Bibi never wore jeans.
Natalie smiled at me.
I smiled back a little.

But not a lot.

"You must be Eleanor," Natalie said.

"Yes," I said.

Then I said,

"Don't ever call me Ellie. Please."

Because Bibi likes to call me Ellie.

"I won't," Natalie said.

"If you don't want me to.

I promise."

Then my dad said,

"Why don't you show Natalie your board games?"

So I showed Natalie our board games.

"I need to warn you about something," she said.

She looked very serious.

"I'm very good at board games," she said.

"You might be able to beat me.

But it will be hard."

"Don't worry," I said.

"I'm good, too."

I am good at board games.

Bibi says she used to let me win,

but now I win all by myself.

I even win the games that are just about luck

and don't take any skill at all.

"You were born under a lucky star," Bibi says.

"Let's play mancala," I said to Natalie.

In mancala you move rocks around in a certain way

and if you have the most rocks at the end

you win.

No one has ever beaten me at mancala.

Natalie didn't beat me, either.

"Look at that," she said.

"I may have met my match."

After that we played lots of different board games.

She won some and I won some.

Then it was time for her to go.

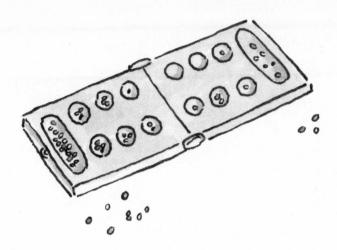

"Next time can we play mancala again?" she asked.

"Okay," I said.

"You can take it home with you now if you want.
To practice."

"Good idea," she said.

Then she went home with our mancala.

CHAPTER FOURTEEN

I decided to sit outside

the very next day

and wait for my letter from Bibi.

"Today?" my mom asked.

"Today," I answered.

"But you just sent your letter to Bibi," my mom said.

"The mail takes time.

It's much too soon to get Bibi's letter back."

"I know," I said.

But I thought,

Maybe it will come.

Maybe.

So I said, "I want to wait anyway."

"Natalie will be here soon," my mom said.

"Maybe she will wait with you."

As soon as Natalie walked in I said,
"I want to sit outside and wait for a letter from Bibi."

My parents must have told Natalie about Bibi.
Because she didn't ask any questions.
She just said, "That sounds nice."

Together we went outside
and sat on a bench across the street from my building
and waited for Bibi's letter.
"You look to the left," I said,
"and I'll look to the right."

So Natalie looked to the left.
And I looked to the right.
And we watched carefully for the mail.

We saw lots of things.
I saw a baby in a stroller
crying and crying and crying
all the way down the block
while its mother said,
"Shh shh shh shh shh."
I figured that baby was tired.

Natalie saw a plastic grocery bag,
hanging from the branch of a tree, swaying.
"Like a magnolia," she said.
"A plastic grocery bag magnolia."

I saw Agnes and her brother walking toward the park.

I waved at Agnes

and she waved back at me.

"That's Agnes from upstairs," I told Natalie.

"You should hear her sing."

Together we counted three,

then four,

then five

joggers rushing by,

their faces drip drip dripping from the heat.

And then we saw the ice-cream truck
turning the corner
playing its tune.

We hopped up
and ran after it
and bought soft ice-cream cones
dipped in chocolate.
We ate those cones up fast,
before they melted.

And when we got back to our bench,
there she was.
The mail carrier lady.
Wheeling her big bag of mail
up the path to our building.
"Wait!" we yelled. "Wait!"

CHAPTER FIFTEEN

The mail carrier lady waited
while we looked both ways
and crossed the street
and ran to her.

"Do you have Bibi's letter?" I asked.
"A letter from Bibi Bholasing?"

"I might," she said.

She looked serious.

"To whom is this letter addressed?" she asked.

"To me," I said.

"Eleanor Abigail Kane."

"It's nice to meet you, Eleanor Abigail Kane,"

the mail carrier lady said.

"I'm Val."

I smiled at Val.

"Do you know your apartment number?" she asked.

"I need it to find the letter."

"It's 2C," I said.

"One moment, please," Val said.

Then she dug through her bag

until she found a stack of mail

labeled 2C.

She took off the rubber bands

and the three of us looked at every letter in that stack.

But there was no letter from Bibi.

"I'm sorry about that," Val said.

"I'll keep a special lookout for it from now on.

I promise."

I knew it was too early for Bibi's letter.

But still.

I wanted my letter from Bibi.

Then Natalie said,

"Maybe it's time to play mancala."

So we went upstairs and played mancala.

I think Natalie might have practiced at home.

Because she did a little better.

But I still won.

CHAPTER SIXTEEN

The next morning
I tried calling my best friend, Pearl.
But she was still away.
Everyone in the world was still away.
Except for me.
So I got grumpy.

When Natalie came,
I said,
"I already hate this day."
"Oh dear," she said.
"But look what I brought."
She held up a bag
and opened it

and showed me
lemons and sugar and a big plastic pitcher.
"If we're going to hate this day," she said,
"then at least let's not get thirsty."
So we squeezed lemons
and scooped sugar
and added water
and stirred
and made a big plastic pitcher
of lemonade.
We made a big sign, too.
We took our pitcher and our sign,
and we set up a lemonade stand,
right next to the bench where we waited for Val.

We poured cups of lemonade for ourselves.
So at least we wouldn't get thirsty.

Then we sold the rest for a nickel.

We decided on a nickel

because *nickel*

rhymes with *pickle*.

The joggers jogged right by us.

But Agnes and her brother each bought a cup.

And one thirsty lady bought two.

That lady drank both of those cups of lemonade

right then and there
all by herself.

While we were waiting for more customers
I asked Natalie,
"Do you remember third grade?"
"A little," she said.
"What's it like?" I asked.
She thought for a second.
"My teacher was named Mrs. Mosley," she said.
"She didn't like my handwriting.
She thought it was too messy."
"Oh," I said.
I thought about my handwriting.
It was pretty messy, too.
"And I think we wrote reports in third grade,"
Natalie said.
"About famous people.
I remember writing one on Neil Armstrong."

"Who's that?" I asked.

"The first person to walk on the moon," Natalie said.

I tried to think of someone famous to write about.

But before I could,

we saw Val.

She was wheeling her bag

up the path to our building.

"Val!" we called, waving. "Val!"

Val waved back

and then turned

and wheeled her big bag right across the street

and over to our stand.

"What a nice way to spend the day," she said.

"Can we check for Bibi's letter?" I asked.
"Just in case?"
"Sure," Val said.
"But I didn't see it earlier."
Then she dug through her bag
and we looked at every 2C letter
but again
no letter from Bibi.

I started to get grumpy.

Then Natalie said,
"Let's get Val some lemonade."
And I poured a cup for Val.
She tried to give us a nickel.
But Natalie said,
"This lemonade is free for Val."
"Let's add that to our sign," I said.
So on our sign

under LEMONADE, ONE NICKEL

I wrote in big letters

FREE FOR VAL.

Val laughed

and thanked us

and wheeled her big bag back across the street

to deliver the rest of her mail.

CHAPTER SEVENTEEN

My mom had to work late the next day.
My dad did, too.
So Natalie stayed late.
And that was bad.

It was bad because
Natalie ran my bath
and checked the water
and checked it again
to make sure it wasn't too hot.
Just like Bibi.
When Bibi stayed late.

And,

before I got in the tub,
Natalie turned back my covers
so my bed was all ready for nighttime.
Just like Bibi.
When Bibi stayed late.

And
I could tell
I could just tell
that after my bath
Natalie planned to read to me
and tuck me in
and kiss me good night
and wish me sweet dreams
and turn down the lights
and tiptoe down the hall.
Just like Bibi.
When Bibi stayed late.

But
Natalie
was not
Bibi.

And
I
wanted
Bibi.

So when Natalie said,
"Your bath is ready,"
I said,
"I don't need a bath.
I'm very clean already."
Natalie looked surprised.
She thought for a minute
and said,
"At least wash your face and hands."

"Fine," I said.

I washed my face and hands

and went in my room.

Then Natalie pulled open my pajama drawer

and said,

"Would you like to pick out some pajamas?"

"No,"

I said.

"I'm not sleeping in pajamas tonight."

Then I slammed that drawer shut.

I had to sleep in something,

so I opened my shirt drawer

and pulled out the very top shirt

and put it on

and turned to Natalie

and said,

"Good night."

"Goodness," Natalie said.

She pointed to the pajama drawer.

"We don't slam drawers," she said.

"Please try again, more gently."

"Fine," I said.

I tried again.

"Are you sure you'll be comfortable in that shirt?"
she asked.

"I'm sure," I said.

"I could read you a bedtime story," she said.

"I'll read to myself," I said.

I got a book

the first book I saw

and climbed with it into my bed.

It was a very big book.

I opened it

and started to read.

That very big book had very long words

that I didn't understand.

But I kept pretending to read.

"Well, then," Natalie said.
"Good night."
She dimmed the lights
and closed the door
and went off down the hall.

I waited a minute.

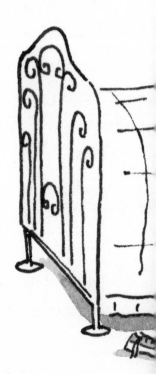

Then I dropped the book on the floor
and put my face in my pillow.
I closed my eyes
and decided
to move
to Florida.

CHAPTER EIGHTEEN

The next morning
Natalie pretended
that last night wasn't bad.
She came in
and slipped off her shoes
and put down her bag
and smiled at me
like she always did.
And then she said,
"Good morning."
"Good morning," I said back.
I hoped she really wasn't mad.
About that drawer.
And the bath.

I couldn't tell if she was.

And I didn't want to ask.

Then I had an idea.

"I'll brush your hair for you," I said.

Sometimes I brush my mom's hair.

And my best friend Pearl's hair, too.

They like it.

"Okay," Natalie said.

I ran to my room

and got my brush.

Which is blue.

My favorite color.

I brought it back to Natalie,
who sat on a chair
and took out her ponytail
and let her hair touch her shoulders.
"Don't worry," I said.
"I'll brush very gently."
Then I brushed her hair very gently.
The way my dad brushes mine sometimes
before he goes to work.
When I had brushed it all, I said,
"What's your favorite color?"
And she said,
"Green."
So I ran back to my room
and got all of the green barrettes I could find.
All three.
Then I made little braids in her hair
and clipped green barrettes at the bottom.
One braid behind each ear

and one down the middle in the back.
"You look beautiful," I said.
She did.
She looked beautiful.
I let her keep those green barrettes.
And she wore them
on those braids
one behind each ear
and one down the middle in the back
the whole rest of the day.

CHAPTER NINETEEN

When the phone rang that night,
I figured it was probably a work call
for my mom.
But she brought me the phone.
"It's for you," she said.
I held the phone to my ear.
"Hello?" I said.
"Eleanor! It's Pearl!" my best friend shouted.
"Pearl!" I shouted back.
"Are you home yet?"
"I wish, wish, wish I was," she said.
"But I'm still in Oregon.
It rains here all the time."
Then she said,

"My face is raining, too.
With tears.
Because I'm missing you."

Pearl talks in poems sometimes.
She's going to be a famous poet someday.
I just know it.

"When will you be back?" I asked.
"Wednesday," she said.
"In the late afternoon.
Mark your calendar!"
"I will," I said. "As soon as I hang up."
"And school starts on Thursday!" Pearl said.
"Will you pick me up on the way?"
"Of course we'll pick you up," I said.

Just then
I remembered

that Pearl didn't know.
About Bibi.

I almost didn't say anything.
Because it felt very hard to say anything.

But I took a deep breath
and I said,
"Bibi moved away."
"She *did*?" Pearl said.
"Yes," I said. "She did."
"Why?" Pearl said.
I told her why.
"You must feel terrible," Pearl said.
"Your heart must feel like a mirror that fell
and shattered in a million pieces."
I thought about that.
"That's exactly right," I said.
"Don't worry," she said.

"I'll be home soon.

I'll cheer you up."

I heard Pearl's mom say something in the background.

"I have to go," Pearl said.

"Wait!" I said.

Because I'd just remembered

that I needed to ask her something.

"Is my handwriting messy?" I asked.

"What?" Pearl said.

"Is my handwriting messy?" I asked again.

"I don't think so," Pearl said.

"I like your handwriting."

Then we hung up.

And right away I went to mark the calendar.

That's when I realized

that it wasn't August anymore.

It was September.

CHAPTER TWENTY

My dad had some time off from work the next day.
So we sat outside together
and waited for Val.
While we waited
I asked him,
"If you had to write about a famous person,
who would you write about?"
"What a great question," he said.
"Let me think."
He did some thinking.
Then he said,
"I might write about Amelia Bloomer."
"Who's that?" I asked.
"She's famous for wearing pants," he said.

"Long ago, when women only wore long, heavy skirts
that were hard to move around in,
Amelia Bloomer thought
they should get to wear pants, too."
"Oh," I said.

I was worried.
I knew nothing at all about famous people.

Then I wondered
if the Bloomer lady's pants
were ever too big.

And then I saw Val,
waving at us.
We hurried to her.
"This is my dad," I said.
"Nice to meet you," Val said.
Then she said,

"One moment, please."
And from the top of her bag,
she pulled out a letter.
"For Miss Eleanor Abigail Kane," she said.
"But don't get too excited."
"Why not?" I asked.
I took the envelope

and looked at it

and saw

why not.

It wasn't from Bibi.

It was from my school.

I opened that thick envelope

and pulled out a long letter.

And while Val delivered the rest of her mail,

I read that long letter with my dad.

It said:

Dear Third Graders,

My name is Mr. Campanelli.

I am your new teacher.

I hope you are having a wonderful summer.

I am getting ready for the start of third grade.

Here are four things I am doing to get ready.

First, I am setting up our classroom.

I want everything to be ready when you get here.

Second, I am going to get a haircut.

Because when my hair gets too long

it gets a little crazy.

Third, I have picked out the shirt I will wear

on our first day.

It is a green-and-blue checked shirt.

It is my favorite shirt.

I wear it on special occasions.

And the first day of school is a very special occasion.

I have enclosed a picture of me in my favorite shirt

so you can know what I'll look like

on the first day of school.

Except my hair will be a little less crazy.

Fourth, I am reading a little every day.

Because reading is a very important part of third grade.

And it is good to get in the habit of reading every day.

I recommend that you start reading a little every day, too,

to help you get ready for third grade.

And, if you want,

you could send me a picture of you.

You could draw it

or take it with a camera.

Whatever you like.

I have included an empty envelope addressed to me.

Just put the picture in and mail it off.

Don't worry about whether the picture will arrive

before school starts.

I will enjoy getting it

whenever it comes.

I look forward to receiving your pictures

and seeing all of you in person

and having a terrific school year.

Your teacher,

Mr. Campanelli

CHAPTER
TWENTY—ONE

I like to draw.

So I decided to draw a picture for Mr. Campanelli.

Before I started drawing,

my dad asked,

"Do you know what you'll wear

on the first day of school?"

"Yes," I said.

I went to my closet

and showed him my white sundress.

It was plain white on top,

with two big orange flowers near the bottom.

"Grandma Sadie gave it to me, remember?" I said.

"That rings a bell," he said.
"All my best clothes are from Grandma Sadie," I said.
"Your grandma has excellent taste," my dad said.
"And you will look wonderful
on your first day of school."

After that I drew a picture
of me in my sundress.
And then
in my very neatest handwriting
I wrote Mr. Campanelli a note.

I wrote:

Dear Mr. Campanelli,
Here is a picture of me
in my first-day-of-school dress.
I drew my hair a little short
because I will get a haircut, too.

I think you will see

my hair and my dress

before you get this letter.

Because the mail takes forever.

Your student,

Eleanor

CHAPTER TWENTY—TWO

When my mom came home
I showed her Mr. Campanelli's letter
and my drawing
and my note.
I had a lot to tell her.
"I have to read every day," I said.
"Good," my mom said.
"There's nothing better than reading."
"And I have to call Pearl in Oregon," I said,
"and read Mr. Campanelli's letter to her.
Because she won't have gotten it."
"No problem," my mom said.

"And I have to get a haircut," I said.

"I just learned that," my mom said. "From your note."

"It has to be a morning haircut," I said.

"So I'm back home before the mail comes."

"I see," my mom said.

"It has to be with Lance," I said.

(I like to get my hair cut by Lance.)

"Of course," my mom said.

"And I have to get it cut just like that," I said,

pointing to my picture.

"Goodness," my mom said, squinting at the picture.

Then she said,

"I will make the perfect appointment.

I promise."

And she did.

She made the perfect appointment.

Then she wrote the date and time for me

on a big piece of paper

and we taped it to my bedroom door.

So we would see it all the time.

And we wouldn't forget.

CHAPTER TWENTY—THREE

The next time Natalie came
she said,
"I brought surprises."
Then she opened her bag
and pulled out a photo album
and a camera.
That photo album was filled
with pictures of flowers.
Giant orange flowers
and little white flowers.
Even bright blue flowers
like the ones I've seen in pictures

of my mom's wedding bouquet.

Natalie knew the names

of every single one of those flowers.

"I took most of these pictures upstate," she said.

"I need more pictures from Brooklyn.

Would you like to go on a walk with me

and take pictures of Brooklyn flowers?"

"I would," I said.

So we went on a walk
and took pictures of Brooklyn flowers.
I'd never noticed before
how many there are
in little gardens
in front of buildings
just off the sidewalks.
Natalie showed me how to hold the camera steady
and where to put my fingers
and when to turn on the flash
and when to turn it off.
After many, many pictures
she said,
"It's time to head back."
So we did.
And right away
we passed Roma Pizza.

Bibi loved Roma Pizza.

I started to think about the walks Bibi and I
used to take
and how she would hold my hand
and say,
"This is the best hand.
I love this hand."

My hand missed Bibi.

I took a deep breath
and said to Natalie,
"I miss Bibi."
Natalie stopped walking
and looked at me.
"Of course you do," she said.
"Of course you miss Bibi.
How long was she your babysitter?"
"My whole life," I said.
"And she was your first babysitter," Natalie said.

"First babysitters are very special."

We started walking again.

Then Natalie said,

"I know I'm not Bibi.

And I'll never be your first babysitter.

But I'll try to be an excellent

second babysitter.

Does that sound okay?"

"Yes," I said.

And it sounded better than okay.

It sounded good.

CHAPTER TWENTY—FOUR

When the telephone rang
on Wednesday
in the late afternoon
I knew it was for me.
"Pearl!" I said.
And she said,
"I called you the second we got in."
Then I heard her mom's voice in the background again.
"I can't really talk," Pearl said.
"I have to unpack and eat and take a bath."
"I'll pick you up tomorrow morning," I said.
"At 8:15 sharp.
Right in front of your building."

"Hurray, hurray, hurray!" Pearl said.

Then we hung up.

Later
I ate, too,
just like Pearl,
and took a bath
and washed my hair,
which Lance had cut just right,
and put on my favorite pajamas.
Then I went to my closet
and took out my white sundress
with the orange flowers on the bottom.
I hung it on my doorknob
so I would find it right away in the morning.
And it wouldn't slow me down.

That night both of my parents tucked me in.
"Such a big day tomorrow," my dad said.
"Are you nervous?" my mom said.
"I'm okay," I said.
But after they dimmed the lights

and left the room
I started worrying.
I worried that I'd be late for Pearl
and late for school
even though I'd put out my dress.
I worried that Mr. Campanelli wouldn't like me.
I worried that I wouldn't get to sit near Pearl.
I worried that my other friends had forgotten me.
I worried that I'd forgotten all my math.
I worried about tests and reports and homework.
I worried about my handwriting.
I worried and worried and worried
until finally I tiptoed through the dark
into my parents' room
and over to their bed,
where they were sleeping.
I tapped my mom on the shoulder.
"I can't sleep," I whispered.
"Mmmmhhhh," she said.

I thought I would have to tap her again.

But then she opened her eyes a little

and scooted over

and lifted up the blanket

for me to crawl in.

She put her arm over me

and I slept right there

right next to my mom

the whole rest of the night.

CHAPTER TWENTY-FIVE

We were right on time for Pearl
and right on time for school.

Mr. Campanelli was at the door of the classroom,
waiting for us, smiling,
with his green-and-blue checked shirt
and his shorter hair
that was not so crazy.

And all my friends were back.
Nora had made necklaces for me and Pearl.
Katie ran up and hugged me.
Adam gave me some gum.

"Let's start the day with some drawing,"
Mr. Campanelli said.
So I sat at a table with Pearl
and Katie and Nora.
And we did some drawing.

Then Mr. Campanelli read us poems
and asked us to write poems of our own.
"Please start your poem
with the words, 'Love Is,'"
he said.
"Think about how you know you love someone
or how you know someone loves you.
And write that down.
Ask me any questions you want.
And don't worry about this a bit.
It's our very first day, after all.
We're just getting warmed up."

So I got paper and a pencil.
And I did some thinking.
Then I wrote my poem.

I wrote:

> Love is calling me Ellie.
>
> Love is ice on my arm.
>
> Love is three green barrettes.
>
> Love is lemonade.

Soon Mr. Campanelli walked around the room
and checked our work.
"An excellent job," he said, when he read my poem.
"But you're making me thirsty!"

He didn't say anything about my handwriting.
So I guess it was fine.
And I thought

I might like third grade.

The rest of the day went very fast.
Soon Natalie was there to pick me up.
"Here," I said, when she came in.
"This is for you."
I handed her one of the pictures I had drawn earlier.
A picture of flowers
in a little garden
just off a sidewalk.
"I love it," Natalie said.
"It's perfect. Thank you."

Then Pearl came over.
I didn't want her to say anything about Bibi.
And she didn't.
Instead she said to Natalie,
"You have the most beautiful hair
I have ever seen."

"Goodness," Natalie said.
She ran her hand over her ponytail.
"Thanks."
Then Natalie smiled at Pearl
and Pearl smiled at Natalie.
And I felt happy.

CHAPTER TWENTY—SIX

Natalie and I walked Pearl and her mom to their building.
Then we headed home.
And as we turned the corner
we saw Val,
who saw us, too,
and raised her arm
and waved and waved
and shouted,
"Come quick, you two!
Run!"
So we ran.
All the way to Val.

CHAPTER TWENTY—SEVEN

When we reached Val
she handed me a letter.
A letter to Miss Eleanor Abigail Kane
from Ms. Bibi Bholasing.
I took that letter
and thanked Val
and ran with Natalie
all the way to my apartment.

Then I wasn't sure what to do.
I wanted to read Bibi's letter by myself.
But I didn't want Natalie to feel bad.

Natalie must have read my mind.

"Would you like to take the letter to your room?"
she asked.
"While I make us a snack?"

I smiled at Natalie
and nodded my head
and went in my room
and sat on my bed
and read my letter from Bibi.

It said:

Dear Eleanor,
I am sorry that your pants are too big.
But I'm sure that will change soon.
Because you are growing so fast.

It is hot here in Florida.

In the afternoons my dad and I now sit on our porch

and wait for the breeze.

We talk about you.

We talk about how smart you are

and how funny you are

and how sweet you are.

I think of you every single day.

You will always be my Ellie.

And I will always be your Bibi.

Even if I am here in hot Florida,

sweating,

and you are far away.

I miss you infinity.

And I love you to the moon and stars and back

and then around again.

All my love,

Bibi

I like reading Bibi's letter.
I read it every single day,
which is good.
Because reading is important for third grade.
I think Bibi's words are beautiful,
like the poems we're reading with Mr. Campanelli.
And like Natalie's hair.
I keep the letter right by my bed
so I see it when I wake up in the morning,
and when I go to sleep at night.

Bibi will always be my first babysitter.
My very special babysitter.
And she will always be my Bibi.
Even if she is waiting for the breeze in Florida,
and I am far away.

ACKNOWLEDGMENTS

I am grateful to the real-life Bibi Bholasing, for inspiring this book and for so much more.

Many thanks as well to Amy Hest and Roslyn Streifer, my dear friends and advisors, for their ceaseless support; Tamar Brazis, my editor, for her graciousness and vision; and Rosemary Stimola, my agent, for making me laugh and for holding my hand.

Most of all, I thank my family, for everything.

Eleanor's story continues in
Like Bug Juice on a Burger.

Here's a sneak peek!

LIKE BUG JUICE ON A BURGER

I hate camp.

I just *hate* it.

I wish I didn't.

But I do.

Being here is worse than

bug juice on a burger.

Or homework on Thanksgiving.

Or water seeping into my shoes.

I want to go home right now.

I really do.

CHAPTER ONE

This all began one day
when Grandma Sadie called me up on the phone.
"I have a wonderful surprise!"
she said.
Right away,
the best possible surprise popped into my mind.
"You're giving us a dog?" I said.
Grandma Sadie was quiet.
Then she said,
"Eleanor, honey.
Your parents don't want a dog."
I knew that.
But I didn't understand it.
"We'd be so happy with a dog,"
I told Grandma Sadie.

"And I'm old enough to take care of it.
I'm nine."
"I know," she said.
"We could name it Antoine," I said.
"I love the name Antoine."
"Then I love it, too," she said.
"But
should we talk about your actual surprise?"
"Oh!" I said.
I'd almost forgotten about that.
"Sure."
"Well," Grandma Sadie said,
"I was just remembering
how much your mother enjoyed
sleepaway camp,
when she was a girl.
I think you'd also enjoy it.
So I'd like to treat you to sleepaway camp
this summer.

Would you like to go?"

"Yes!" I said. "I would!"

I really meant it, too.

"My friend Katie went last summer," I said.

"Every single day she ate M&M's.

And rode horses.

And jumped on a floating trampoline."

"How marvelous!" Grandma Sadie said.

"She got great at diving, too," I said.

"They gave her trophies."

"Let's get you started winning trophies,"
Grandma Sadie said.
"I'll call your mom's camp right away.
Camp Wallumwahpuck."
She did, too.
She called that camp with the crazy name
right away.

She also sent me a photograph, in the mail.
An old camp picture of my mom
when she was a girl.
She's standing outside a small white cabin,
wearing a backpack
and hugging a rolled-up, puffy sleeping bag.
She looks so happy.

I taped that picture to the wall by my bed
and looked at it night after night
before the start of summer.

All those nights,
I believed I'd be happy at Wallumwahpuck, too.
I really did.

ABOUT THE AUTHOR

Julie Sternberg is the author of the Eleanor series, which includes *Like Pickle Juice on a Cookie*, *Like Bug Juice on a Burger*, and *Like Carrot Juice on a Cupcake*. Formerly a public interest lawyer, Julie is a graduate of The New School's MFA program in writing for children. She lives in Brooklyn, New York.

ABOUT THE ILLUSTRATOR

Matthew Cordell is the illustrator of the Eleanor series and the author and illustrator of *hello! hello!*, *Wish*, and many other books for children. He lives in the suburbs of Chicago.